Callie's Kitten

Adèle Geras

Illustrated by

Tony Ross

A Dell Yearling Book

Published by
Dell Yearling
an imprint of
Random House Children's Books
a division of Random House, Inc.
New York

First American Edition 2003
First published in Great Britain by Young Corgi Books, Transworld Publishers Ltd, a division of the Random House Group Ltd, in 1998

Illustrations by arrangement with Transworld Publishers Ltd, a division of the Random House Group Ltd

---

ISBN: 0-440-41816-X (pbk.) ISBN: 0-385-90081-3 (lib. bdg.)
Printed in the United States of America
April 2003
10 9 8 7 6 5 4 3 2 1
OPM

Contents

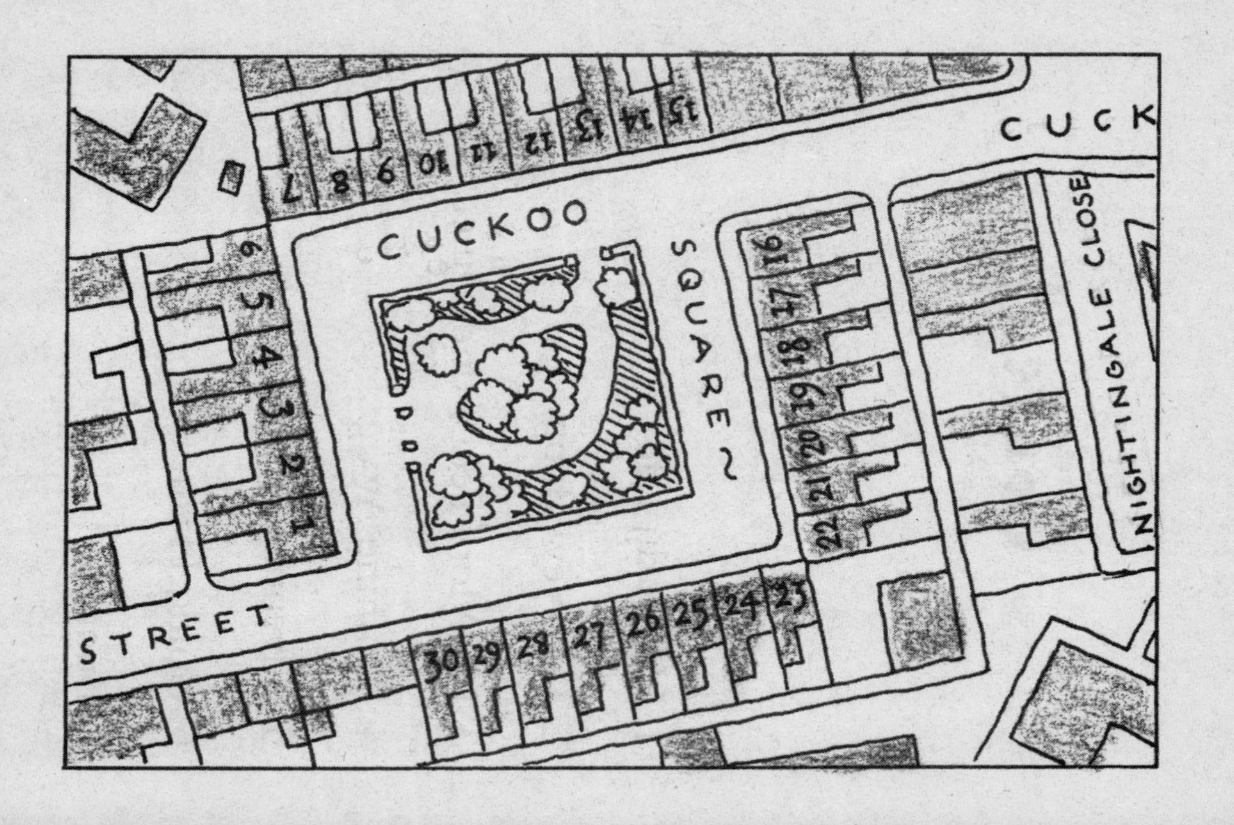
CUCK
NIGHTINGALE CLOSE
CUCKOO SQUARE~
STREET
1
2
3
4
5
6
7
8
9
10
11
12
13
14
15
16
17
18
19
20
21
22
23
24
25
26
27
28
29
30

1.
My Early Life

"Callie! Callie! Wake up! You're dreaming."

I opened my eyes and there was Blossom, pushing her nose against mine.

"You were dreaming again," said Perkins.

"And growling in your sleep," said Geejay. "We thought we should wake you up at once."

Blossom, Perkins, and Geejay are my greatest friends among the cats who live in Cuckoo Square.

"Oh, my padded paws!" I said. "I was having a dreadful nightmare. I was locked in a very dark room, and I didn't know where *you* all were, or what had happened to our square, or our people, and I had no idea if I was going to find any food ever again. Thank you for waking me up."

"Come and sit down over here," said Blossom, and she led me to one of our favorite spots, the sheltered place under the rhododendron bushes. Snow had fallen on Cuckoo Square. Nobody at all was sitting on the benches and all the trees were bare and dusted with white, so the garden belonged to us cats. A little sunshine had crept through the branches and we were all quite comfortable.

Blossom began to lick herself all over. It is difficult for a cat to talk and wash at the same time, so I was left alone with my thoughts, and I'm sorry to say that they weren't very happy ones.

Of all the cats who live in Cuckoo Square, I am the only one who has been rescued. The Andersons found me in a cat shelter. I am four years old, and my early life was not happy. This is the reason, I think, for my nightmares. I seem to dream far more than any of my friends. I was much too young to be separated from my mother when I was taken away from her. I remember her kind black-and-white face only very dimly. Sometimes I imagine that she looked very like dear Blossom: fluffy and plump and beautiful, and perhaps my father was a ginger tom like Geejay, because I am a calico cat, and my fur is a patchwork of white and ginger and black.

"You look," said Blossom one day, "like one of those cat statues that live on people's mantelpieces. Your eyes are such a pretty color, and I do love that black patch."

I cannot bring to mind anything at all of the first home I went to as a tiny kitten, but I *do* remember how I left it. Someone put me into a box. It was a small, dark space with cardboard walls, and though I meowed as hard as I knew how and scratched at the side of my prison

with my little claws, the box stayed shut. Then I was bumped up and down, and kept sliding from one side of the darkness to the other. After that, everything was silent. I slept for a short while, but then I noticed that the cardboard I was lying on was soaking wet, and, what was even worse, I couldn't find anything to eat or drink. If a kind person had not chanced to see the box I was imprisoned in lying in a puddle on the pavement, I would certainly have died.

The lady who found me took me to the cat shelter, where I was dried and brushed and fed and stroked and put to live in a warm cage, next door to a rather grumpy gray cat who hardly ever felt like talking to me.

But I was so relieved to be out of the dark and the cold, and so happy not to be hungry anymore, that I thought the shelter was all a cat could wish for. Then one day as I was lying with my eyes closed, I felt a small finger stroking my nose through the bars of the cage. I opened my eyes and there was a little boy staring at me.

"This kitten," he said. "I want this kitten."

"She's very young," said his mother. "She's probably not even house-trained."

"Don't care!" said the boy. "I want this one."

"She *is* sweet," said his mother. "Calico cats are so pretty."

"Callie Cat," said the boy. "She's my Callie Cat."

"Calico." His mother smiled at him.

"That's what I said," he told her. "Callie. That's her name."

And so I came to Cuckoo Square. The little boy who found me and gave me my name is seven years old now. He is called David. His parents' names are Liz and Nick Anderson, and my home, at No. 18, is Cat Paradise—or it was until a very short time ago, when David told me that there would soon be a new baby coming to live in our house. The moment I heard this, I went straight into the square to share the news with my friends.

"Oh, my waving whiskers!" I said. "You'll never guess what's coming to live in our house."

"A goldfish?" said Blossom.

"A pet bird, perhaps?" Perkins suggested.

"Is it a puppy?" Geejay asked.

"No," I said. "It's a baby."

2. The New Baby

"They are bringing the baby home from the hospital today," I told my friends. "I've been thinking about it and I don't really understand why my people should want one."

"They like to cuddle babies," said Blossom, "and feed them all the time and carry them around."

"They do all those things," I said, "to me."

"Perhaps," said Perkins, "David wants a brother or a sister he can talk to. As the Furry Ancestors say: 'Words are for humans, purring is for cats.'"

"David thinks words are for cats too," I said. "He often talks to me. I understand everything he says."

"But," said Geejay, "does he understand everything you say to *him*?"

"Not everything," I had to admit. "No."

Perkins smoothed his whiskers with one paw. "The Furry Ancestors say: 'Silence flees the house when a baby enters it.' Babies are extremely noisy. There'll be no more peace and quiet for you, Callie."

"Then I'd better go and have my lunch before they get back."

I made my way into the house through the cat-flap. There was a lady in the kitchen whom I had seen before. I recognized her smell and her voice, but I'd forgotten exactly who she was.

"Hello, Callie, dear," she said. "Do you remember me? I'm Rita, David's Nan. Liz's mother. Follow me. They left me in charge of your lunch."

Oh, my fluffy forepaws! Of course I remembered Nan. The minute she began to cut up a piece of fish for me, I remembered how fond of her I was. She chatted away to me all the time, and the food always improved greatly whenever she came to stay. Every time she passed the fish market, she would go in and buy a little treat for me: a piece of salmon skin, say, or a few prawns.

"So, Callie," she said as I was eating. "A new baby, eh? What do you think of that? No more peace and quiet for poor old Puss!"

It was a little worrying. Perkins had said exactly the same thing, but I had been hearing quite different stories from David.

"Callie," he said to me before the baby was born, "I'm going to have a sister. Or a brother. I'm so excited. It'll be someone I can play with. Someone I can talk to."

I must have looked a little hurt, because he added quickly: "I know I can play with you, Callie. Of course I can. But I'll be able to teach my baby things, won't I?"

I turned my back on him and began to lick my front paws very energetically. I knew exactly what he meant. He'd tried to teach me to read once, propping pieces of paper with black marks on them against the wall and saying: "*A*, Callie—that's the letter *A*. It says *A*, like *apple*. *A* is for *apple* . . . and that's *B*—*B* is for *book*."

I think he was offended when I sniffed these pieces of paper and wandered off to look for something more interesting to do. If I had a kitten, I thought, I'd teach it how to hunt mice and other small creatures, and all the very best ways to lick the hard-to-reach parts of the body: useful, practical things that would make its life easier. I wished that a kitten were coming to the house, instead of a baby.

"Come and see where our baby will live, Callie," he said to me just before everyone left for the hospital. He picked me up and carried me upstairs. "I'll put you down just while I open the door," he said.

I already knew that something

interesting had been happening in that room. Nick had been spending a lot of time hammering on pieces of wood, and when he went on to paint the walls, all sorts of strange smells had come to my nostrils. Now, as David and I looked in from the corridor, I could see that everything was colored pale yellow. The new curtains at the window were scattered with flowers. I looked for a long time at some fishes hanging from the ceiling on long black threads, and David laughed at me.

"They're not *real* fishes," he told me. "It's called a mobile, and it's for the baby to look at while it lies in its crib."

The minute I saw the crib, I longed to jump up and settle myself on the fluffy white blankets I could see there, which looked as soft and warm as cotton wool, or clouds. But why were there wooden railings around the crib? I was sure that the baby would be delighted to have me curled up at the end of its bed. There was nothing for it. I would have to try to squeeze between the bars. David must have seen me crouching down, ready to leap, and he picked me up and hugged me to him.

"Oh, no, Callie, you must never, ever go on the baby's bed. That's not allowed. Mum says so. Come on, let's go back down now." He carried me out of the room and shut the door. "I'm closing it, Callie," he said, "so that you won't sneak in while I'm not looking."

I walked downstairs feeling a little put out. Never in all my time in the Anderson house had I ever been forbidden to do anything.

Now here I was, waiting for the baby to come home, and Nan was watching me eat my lunch.

"Any minute now," she told me. "They'll soon be here with the baby. It's a lovely little girl."

3.
No More Peace and Quiet

The new baby is not what I expected at all. Her name is Celia.

"I'm going to call her Sis," David told me, "because she's my sister."

She is bald, and very wrinkled and pink, and she looks nothing like any little girl I've ever seen. Human babies are even more helpless than kittens. They have to be fed and

washed and carried round in people's arms, because (and I find this amazing) they cannot walk or crawl, nor can they speak properly. This baby lies wherever Liz or Nick or Nan put her, and the noises that come out of her tiny mouth are earsplitting: the moment she begins to wail, I run away. She cries a great deal, it's true, but there are times when she is lying quietly sleeping, and I look at her and think: "Oh, my twitching tail! How delightful it would be to lick her and groom her. Then she could be *my* baby and not just David's."

From the day she arrived, there have been visitors knocking at our door. Each time I find a comfortable chair to lie on, a human appears, lifts me off it, and puts me down on the floor. I usually run to David's room and jump on his bed, but there's no peace there either these days. David keeps coming in to disturb me.

"Look," he said today. "All the visitors are bringing presents for Sis, and lots of them have given me one too. Look at this!"

David has always shared his toys with me, and he's often tried to get me to join in his games, but I've never found them very interesting. Now he showed me his gifts and then left them lying on top of the bed next to me, taking up space I would have liked to stretch out in. I sniffed at toy trains, and tiny creatures that looked like humans but were hard all over and smelled

very strange. I examined wooden boats and big cardboard boxes that seemed interesting, but which unfortunately were firmly closed. I decided to go out to the square and avoid the visitors for a while.

I found Perkins sitting in the sheltered porch of his house.

"Callie," he said. "I am surprised to see you. You are a brave cat to venture out in this cold weather."

"You are brave, too, Perkins," I said.

"Ah, but I am used to it," he said. "I've seen many snowy winters. I find them bracing."

"Our house is full of visitors," I told him, "and they have all brought gifts for the baby. I can't imagine why, because she cannot possibly play with them."

"It is a tradition," said Perkins. "It's good manners to greet a new baby with a present."

"Oh, my bushy back paws!" I said. "I'd better look around for something, even though there isn't much to be found in the middle of winter."

"How true!" Perkins said. "As the Furry Ancestors say: 'Hunter and hunted both like to keep warm.' "

"I shall go and look for something under those trees. Goodbye, Perkins."

"Goodbye, Callie," he said, and made his way solemnly down the steps and along the path that led to his cat-flap.

I had only been looking for a few

minutes when I found a little bird lying at the foot of one of the trees in the square. I didn't have to hunt it because it was lying very still. I patted it and pushed it with my front paws, and it wouldn't stir. It was definitely a dead bird.

"What luck!" I said to myself. "I shall pick it up and give it to Sis."

As I made my way home with the bird in my mouth, I imagined everyone exclaiming and telling me that I was the best and kindest cat in the world. They would stroke me and praise me, and probably give me a delicious treat to eat. I made my way to the cat-flap as quickly as I could and pushed my way in. Everyone was in the living room admiring the baby, who was being cuddled in Liz's arms. They were drinking tea and eating slices of cake. I trotted over to the fireplace and dropped my gift on the hearthrug. Two of the ladies shrieked and jumped up, dropping their plates and sending cake crumbs flying all over the carpet. Nick came over to

me at once, and he was frowning and looked crosser than I'd ever seen him.

"Naughty Callie!" he said. "You know we don't allow dead birds in the house." He picked it up on the coal shovel and walked quickly out of the room.

I followed him, feeling very hurt. He didn't understand what I was trying to tell him: "It's not an ordinary bird," I meowed. "It's a present for the baby."

He took no notice but wrapped the bird up in a plastic bag and opened the back door to throw it into the trash bin. As he left the kitchen, he said to me: "Stay in here, Callie. I'm going to close the door behind me. I don't want to see you again till all the guests have gone."

I thought David would come and visit me in the kitchen and tell me he understood. We had always been such friends. He spoke to me more than he ever did to anyone else. I was sure he would be kind to me, but he never came, and in the end I fell asleep with my head resting on the knitted snake that was lying pushed up against the back door to keep the drafts out.

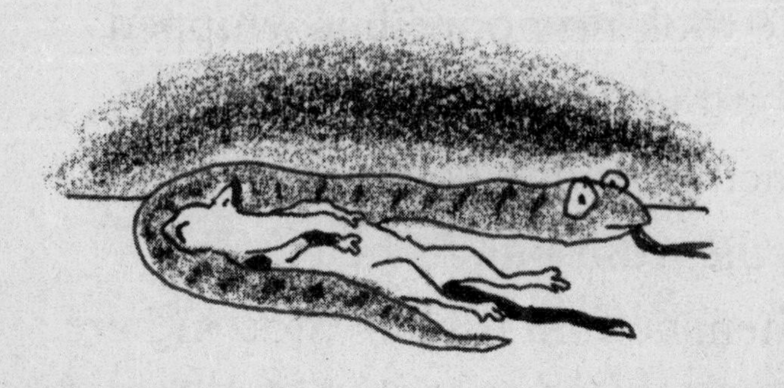

4.
Running Away

Later that afternoon, I went out to the square because I longed to talk to someone. Geejay was there, and I told him all my troubles.

"I'm feeling very neglected," I said. "No one takes any notice of me any longer. I might just as well be invisible. Do you know, this morning, I had to meow loudly for a good few minutes before Nan suddenly noticed that my bowl was quite empty, and I was waiting for my breakfast?"

"You should teach them a lesson," Geejay said. "If you ran away, they'd all miss you. You can be sure of that."

"I'm *not* sure at all," I said. "And in any case, I'd be frightened. Where would I go? Where would I find food? Wouldn't it be dangerous? And it's so cold. . . ."

"You could find somewhere to hide and go back later. Or you could find someone else to live with. Another family."

"Oh, my tuna tidbits!" I cried, shocked at the idea. "No. 18 is my home. David is my person, and the whole family is my family."

"Of course," said Geejay, "we would all miss you if you *really* ran away, but disappearing for a little while is often a good idea. I've done it myself, usually on hunting expeditions."

“But you’re brave,” I said, “and I’m a scaredy-cat.”

Geejay smiled. I said goodbye to him and went back to the house. It was getting colder and colder.

Once I was indoors, I went upstairs to look for David. The door of the baby’s room was open. I looked in and saw Liz, busy dressing her for the night. David was helping

his mother, handing her things. The crib was empty. I knew I wasn't allowed in the crib, but I thought no one would mind if I curled up in there for a moment, just till Sis was ready to sleep. I knew I would have to leave the crib then, but I remembered how lonely I sometimes was when I was a tiny kitten, and I thought: It's a pity I can't stay here. I'm sure Sis would be happy to have a furry creature keeping her company, whatever they say.

No one was looking, so I jumped up and settled myself on the blankets. When Liz turned round and saw me sleeping, she began to shriek as though I were some kind of monster.

"Callie!" she shrieked. "Out! Get her out, David! Quick! Oh, you wicked cat! You *know* you're not allowed in this room. Out! Out!"

She walked toward the crib, scowling, and I fled. David ran after me, clapping his hands and saying horrible things like "Shoo!" and "Go away!" He chased me right into the kitchen, where Nan was peeling potatoes.

"Leave poor Callie alone, David," she said.

"She was in Sis's crib," said David. "Mum says she'll leave mud from her paws there, or even fleas. Imagine if a flea bit Sis!"

Every word he said felt to me like a kick. I was hurting somewhere deep inside my head and all through my body. The first time I'd seen David crying, I didn't understand why his face was so damp and his nose was so wet, nor why he was wailing so loudly. I was frightened, but Liz had explained to me: "He's crying, Callie, because he's feeling unhappy. Sometimes it makes you feel better."

I remembered those words now and wished that cats could cry. There are all sorts of other sounds

I could have made—yowling or screeching or meowing—but I felt too sad to say anything. I sat on the windowsill for a long time, looking out at the square. The sky was a purply gray, and as I watched, more snowflakes drifted down to the ground like thousands of white moths. Blossom, Perkins, and Geejay were nowhere to be seen. It was too cold. All sensible cats would be staying very close to the radiator on an evening like this. I thought:

Nobody in this house loves me anymore. Still, if someone had said something pleasant to me, anything at all, I would never have decided to follow Geejay's advice.

Instead, Nick came into the kitchen for supper and said to Liz: "We must lock Callie in the kitchen at night from now on. We can't take the risk of her getting into Celia's room."

I could hardly believe my ears. For the first time since coming to Cuckoo Square, I wouldn't be able to sleep on David's bed. That was when I made my mind up. I would be brave. I would run away.

5.
Adventures in the Dark

I waited till the next afternoon. Everyone was in the living room, watching the television. It was already dark and the snow had stopped falling. There was a bright moon in the sky. Don't be scared, Callie, I said to myself. I would soon be back. And when I was, they'd be so pleased to see me that they would all

start being nice to me straightaway, and they'd never lock me in the kitchen overnight again. I had realized that there were many places where I could hide from the worst of the cold. Sometimes the shed in Perkins's garden was open during the evening, and so was the garage belonging to Geejay's family. Also, it wouldn't be long before David began to wonder where I was, and then they would all come looking for me. I was certain of it.

I pushed the cat-flap open and slipped out as quietly as I could. I hadn't realized quite how cold it was. Cuckoo Square was deserted. The ground under the rhododendron bushes had frozen hard, and the snow

I walked across made my paws wet and chilly. I went off to look for somewhere warm to hide, but nothing was open in any of the houses that were familiar to me. The moonlight made the shadows almost black, and things that looked quite ordinary in the daylight loomed over me like monsters. Cars had turned into enormous animals crouching in the snow, and trash bins towered over my head like mountains.

I heard strange noises, too: the nearly doglike barking of a fox, and the groaning of trees as they bent in the wind. There were no people anywhere.

When I passed Blossom's house, I jumped up onto the windowsill. The curtains in the front room were tightly closed, but there was a thin line of light showing, and when I pushed my nose right up against the glass, I found that I could see quite a lot of Blossom's living room. There she was, lying on the sofa next to Miles, her favorite person. Her back was touching his legs, and every now and then he stroked her and I could see the tips of her ears trembling.

"Blossom!" I meowed. "Oh, my frosty fur! It's me, Callie!"

She couldn't hear me because the television was on and music was playing. I didn't really want her to see me. I knew that if I went into her house, her people would take me home at once, and I wasn't ready to go back yet. Never mind, Callie, I said to myself. It won't be long now.

David will be coming down for his tea, and he'll notice that I've gone, and he'll start to look for me, and when he can't find me in any of our special places, he'll start to cry. At first, I thought, no one will pay much attention because it's Sis's bath time, and then it'll be time to feed her and put her to bed, but after that, maybe even Liz and Nick will see I'm not in the house, and then they'll open the back door and call my name, and when I don't appear, that's when they'll start looking for me.

I jumped down from the windowsill. Blossom had just started washing, licking her back paw and the end of her fluffy tail. She and Miles looked so warm and cozy that it made me feel sad to look at them. I went trotting along the pavement, trying to keep my feet warm. Find a shelter, Callie, I said to myself, or you'll be frozen solid before anyone finds you.

I made my way down Nightingale Close, one of the little roads leading off the square. Most of the houses here had their curtains drawn too, and there were hardly any comforting golden patches of light shining out onto the pavement. For the first time in many months, I was leaving my own territory. I sniffed. Something smelled good and I was very hungry. I followed my nose and went down an unfamiliar garden path toward a trash bin. It had been tipped over on its side, and alongside the delicious aroma of old chicken bones I could smell fox. This is where he was, I thought, and sniffed again, making sure that his odor was fading and he had gone. I started to eat, and even though I was damp and unhappy and my paws were aching from the cold, I think that chicken was one of the

tastiest meals I've ever eaten. I looked around. The house had a garage, and the garage was open. I won't have to stay here long, I thought. They'll be calling me any minute now and coming to look for me.

It was clear from the smells in the garage that there was a dog who spent a lot of time in it. I hoped he was safely indoors and wouldn't come out. I didn't feel like being chased, and I felt even less like chasing. There were some rags in the corner, and I made a nest in them and fell asleep.

6. Going Home

When I woke up, I was stiff and chilly. I stretched myself and gave my paws a lick. How long had I been sleeping? I jumped up onto a shelf under the garage window to look at the moon. It had traveled so far across the sky that I knew it was the very middle of the night. David, I said to myself, must be fast asleep

by now. So must Liz and Nick. It was hours and hours since I'd left the house, and not one single person had missed me. I'm going to leave this place, I thought. I'm going to find a new home where everyone will love me properly and notice when I'm not there. I crept over to the garage door, but someone had closed it. How was I going to get out? I looked along the walls for a gap I could crawl through, but I couldn't find one. "Oh, my clutching claws!" I said, and I shivered with dread. "This is terrible! It's exactly like one of my nightmares. I'm in a dark place with no food and no way out."

I began to meow as loudly as I could. "Help!" I said. "Please come and find me and I promise I'll never run away again. And I'll never jump into Sis's crib! And I'll only snuggle up to her if I'm allowed to. Please! Please come and let me out!"

Nobody answered. Nobody came. I felt more miserable than I'd ever felt in my life. I crept back to my bed in the garage and stared at the darkness. They don't love me, I thought. They don't care about me. Nobody even notices if I'm there or not. I sat very still and quiet for a long time, thinking.

Don't be a silly cat, Callie, I said to myself after a while. You might as well sleep till morning. Everyone's in bed now, and no one can hear you. You can try again in the morning when they're all awake.

I put my head between my paws and fell asleep. I don't know how long I slept. I was dreaming. I dreamed that someone was calling

my name, somewhere very far away, so far away that I could hardly hear it. Then it grew louder in my dream, and I woke up. I could still hear it.

"Callie! Callie!" someone was shouting. "Come back, Callie!" It was David.

"Callie!" said another voice. "Where are you, Callie?" That was Nan.

At last, I thought joyfully. They're looking for me! And they sound really sad. But how can I make them hear me? Will they come this way? I ran to the door of the garage and meowed and meowed as loudly as I knew how. "David!" I said. "I'm here! Please come and find me. Please!"

They *were* getting closer. I could hear them now, and David was weeping. I'd heard him crying many times, but this was different. He sounded so heartbroken that I suddenly felt ashamed that I was the one who'd made him feel like that. What an unkind cat I was to *want* to make him worry!

"Oh, Nan," David was sobbing, "what if we never find her? What if she's lost and never comes back? I love my Callie. Where is she? She's been out all night and it's so cold . . . what if she's frozen to death?"

I couldn't bear to hear him sounding so unhappy for one more second. "Here!" I cried. "Come here and find me—you're so close. Please come here!"

"Listen!" said Nan. "I can hear something. Callie? Callie, is that you?"

"Yes, yes, it's me," I called. "I'm in this garage."

"She's here, David," Nan shouted. "Callie's in here."

The door of the garage opened

suddenly, and there was David. "Oh, Callie!" he said, and picked me up and squashed me against his coat. "Callie . . . oh, I'm so happy to see you! Don't ever, ever run away again. Promise." He pushed his face into my neck, and soon my fur was damp with his tears.

"Come on, David. And Callie," said Nan. "Let's go in now. This cat will be needing some food and some nice warm milk, and I expect you could do with some hot chocolate, David. I know that's what I fancy."

I began to purr. When we reached the kitchen, Liz and Nick jumped up from where they were sitting at the table.

"Callie, darling," said Liz, and she took me out of David's arms and cuddled me as though I were her very own baby.

"Look, Callie," said Nan. "We've got some prawns for you and some nice fresh milk."

That was the best meal of my whole life. David sat beside me and

stroked my back until I'd finished the last delicious pink morsel. He bent down and whispered in my ear. "Callie," he said. "You must promise me never to run away again. Do you promise?"

I was too full of food to say very much, but I purred at him and rubbed my head against his hand. He picked me up and carried me to his room, and put me on his bed to sleep. As I closed my eyes, I thought: They're not going to close the kitchen door at night. Not anymore. They'll make a big fuss of me from now on. I'll have lovely dreams tonight. I know I will.

7.
Buggins

I slept for so long that by the time I woke up, it was a new day and a much warmer one. There was fresh food in my dish. I finished my breakfast and jumped up onto the windowsill. Most of the snow had melted away. I knew my friends would be out in the square. I hadn't seen Blossom for a long time, and besides, I wanted to tell them all about my adventures. Where was David? I went into every room in the house, but it was empty. They've gone, I thought. They've all gone and they've left me here all on my own. They NEVER all go out together. Why have they left me by

myself? Even though I was in my own house, I was frightened. What if they never came back? What would I do? I must go and ask my friends' advice, I thought.

I pushed through the cat-flap and ran into the garden. I found Perkins, Geejay, and Blossom gathered in a small, sunny spot near one of the trees. They all listened politely as I told my story.

"Well," Blossom said when I had finished, "I think it was very brave of you. I would never dare to do such a thing. Mind you, I'm not as young as I was. Perhaps if I were your age . . . and I *am* sorry I didn't see you on my windowsill. You must have felt so lonely. And how lucky that you were found! Imagine if they hadn't walked down Nightingale Close. You could have been locked up for days."

"I know," I said. "I was so happy to be home, but now my people have disappeared. What will I do if they never come back?"

"They *are* back," said Perkins. "That is their car coming into the square, is it not?"

"Oh, my succulent salmon!" I said. "It is! I shall go inside and wait for them."

★★★

They crowded into the hall. Nick was carrying a cardboard box. I recognized it at once and shivered. It had a handle at the top to make it easier to carry, and it was exactly like the one I had been put into when I was a tiny kitten. I thought:

They're going to shut me up in it and throw me away, and then I heard a tiny scrabbling noise from inside the box, and a thin voice crying and crying. Even though I'd never had a litter of my own, I knew at once that it was a kitten. Suddenly, I felt excited and I could feel my heart beating very loudly.

"Don't cry, little one," I meowed, as loudly as I could. "They'll let you out soon."

"Here you are," said Liz, and she opened the top of the box. "Callie, this is Buggins."

Buggins was the smallest, blackest kitten I'd ever seen. He was also very fast on his feet. He shot out of the box, skittered across the kitchen, and disappeared behind the boiler.

"His mother was run over," David said to me. "All her kittens were taken to the shelter. They're only about four weeks old. I told the lady at the shelter that you wanted a baby of your own. You do, don't you, Callie? I think that was why you ran away, wasn't it? I had a baby, so you wanted one as well. I could see that you wanted to help look after Sis and we never let you. Mum thinks I'm mad, but I said you needed a kitten to be your baby."

I sighed. David was being kind, I knew he was, but when I remembered how the Andersons had pampered me when I was younger, I felt sad all over again. They would look after Buggins and forget all about

me. They'd grow to love him. What if they loved him best? Better than me? What then? I settled down on my favorite kitchen chair and pretended to go to sleep. Let's see them make him come out, I thought. I waited for the coaxing to begin. I waited for them to put out tasty morsels of this and that. To my amazement, however, they all left the room.

I listened, with my ears pricked, for noises from behind the boiler. Nothing. Silence. I don't care, I said to myself. Let the creature sulk if he wants to, and then I thought: He ran over there so fast that he may have hurt his little paws. It's a new house for him. He'll be frightened. He's lost his mother. I jumped down from the chair.

"Buggins?" I said.

Silence.

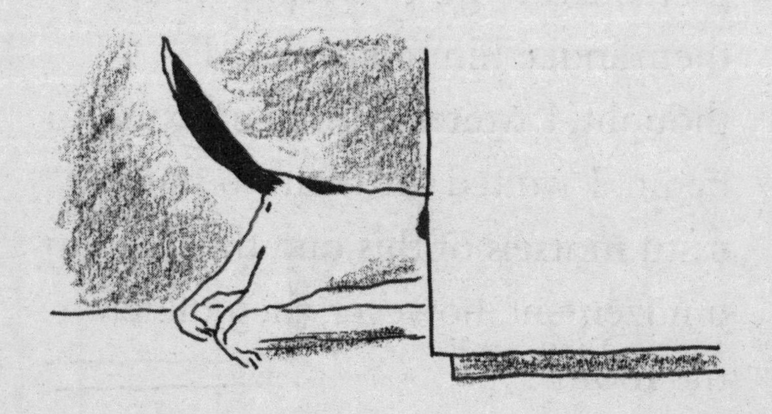

"Buggins? You can come out now, dear. There's no one here but me. I won't hurt you. My name is Callie. Come out and I'll give you a lick."

The smallest black nose I'd ever seen peeped out at me. Two big yellow eyes blinked at me. Buggins said: "Will you really lick me? My mother used to lick me, but I can't find her."

I didn't want Buggins to feel sad in his new home, so I just said: "Have some food first, and then I'll give you a good wash. I expect you're hungry."

"I'm always hungry," said Buggins. He followed me to my bowl and finished every scrap of food in seconds.

"They'll give you your own bowl, I'm sure," I said, "when they see what a good eater you are. I was a little fussy when I was a kitten."

When Buggins had finished, I began to lick him. It felt strange at first, grooming another cat, but it made me feel like a real mother. The more I licked Buggins, the more affectionate I felt toward him. The best thing of all was that he loved it and began to purr.

"Oh, my cuddlesome kitten," I said, "you've got a very loud purr for one so young."

"Is that good?" he asked.

"It's excellent," I told him. "You will grow up to be a fine cat."

"I'm going to be a hunter," Buggins announced. "Can we go hunting now?"

"Certainly not. You're much too young to be allowed outside. Also, it's far too cold. And there are all sorts of things I have to teach you. Do you know about litter boxes?"

"They had one at the shelter," said Buggins. "Can we go exploring? In the house?"

"Yes," I said. "We can go everywhere except in the baby's room."

"What's a baby?" Buggins asked.

"You'll see," I said. "Now come along with me."

We left the kitchen together. Buggins managed to find his way into every tiny corner, sniffing at everything, rubbing his chin all over the furniture and learning his way around the house. When we got to David's room, I picked Buggins up by the scruff of the neck and jumped up on the bed.

"And now, my sleepy little scamp, it's time to snooze," I told him. "You'll be able to explore again later."

Buggins yawned. "Will you be my mother?"

"Would you like me to be?" I asked.

"Yes, please."

"Then I will be. Close your eyes now."

He curled up into a furry black ball, and I licked the tips of his ears and went to sleep beside him. Looking after kittens was very tiring.

★★★

During the next few days, I only managed to slip out and chat to my friends when Buggins was asleep.

"We are all looking forward to meeting him," said Perkins.

"He'll be out in a few weeks, after he's had his vaccinations. And he wants to be a hunter. Geejay, I shall advise him to learn from you."

"And do the Andersons make a big fuss of him?" Blossom wanted to know.

"They treat us just the same now, but they let me look after him all by myself at first. We even share the same food bowl. Now they call us the kits. David plays with us all the time because he says kittens are more interesting than babies."

"What about the baby?" asked Perkins. "Is she still being a nuisance?"

"She's a little noisy sometimes, but only when she's hungry. Buggins is just the same. He can meow most annoyingly when he's kept waiting for his food, so I sympathize with Sis now. I'm also very busy. I spend ages running around after Buggins, making sure he stays out of mischief—and oh, my nuzzling nostrils, he's the most inquisitive creature you can imagine."

"He sounds," said Geejay, "as though he'll make a very good hunter."

I went home feeling that nowhere would I ever find a better place to live than Cuckoo Square. I had a good home, and good friends. I had my own loving family, and now I had little Buggins. I couldn't think of anything else in the whole world that I wanted, except perhaps some chicken and tuna in my dish, and I was sure I would find that as well, unless dear Buggins had woken up and cleaned out our bowl. I slipped through the cat-flap, calling out his name.

About the Author

Adèle Geras has published more than eighty acclaimed books for children and young adults, including *My Grandmother's Stories,* which won the Sydney Taylor Award in 1991. Her most recent novel is *Troy,* which was a *Boston Globe–Horn Book* Honor Book. She is married, has two grown-up daughters, and lives in Manchester, England. She loves books, movies, all kinds of theater, and, of course, cats.

About the Illustrator

Tony Ross is the award-winning illustrator of several books for children, including the Amber Brown series by Paula Danziger. He lives with his family in Cheshire, England.

After a picnic lunch outside, everyone returned to the kitchen to put the finishing touches on their peppermint brownies. Then Chef Giorgio walked around tasting samples.

"Mmm, *magnifico!*" he said to Chloe, who blushed and grinned with pleasure. "Yes, very good, but perhaps a touch less flour next time," he said to Cristin.

He reached George's workstation. "Little Giorgio! Let's see what you have created!" he said with a big smile.

George cut into her pan of brownies and handed the chef a big piece. He popped it into his mouth . . .

. . . and his smile instantly vanished. "*Yuck!* This is the worst peppermint brownie I have ever tasted!" he cried.

Cooking Camp Disaster

Join the CLUE CREW
& solve these other cases!

#1 *Sleepover Sleuths*

#2 *Scream for Ice Cream*

#3 *Pony Problems*

#4 *The Cinderella Ballet Mystery*

#5 *Case of the Sneaky Snowman*

#6 *The Fashion Disaster*

#7 *The Circus Scare*

#8 *Lights, Camera . . . Cats!*

#9 *The Halloween Hoax*

#10 *Ticket Trouble*

#11 *Ski School Sneak*

#12 *Valentine's Day Secret*

#13 *Chick-napped!*

#14 *The Zoo Crew*

#15 *Mall Madness*

#16 *Thanksgiving Thief*

#17 *Wedding Day Disaster*

#18 *Earth Day Escapade*

#19 *April Fool's Day*

#20 *Treasure Trouble*

#21 *Double Take*

#22 *Unicorn Uproar*

#23 *Babysitting Bandit*

#24 *Princess Mix-up Mystery*

#25 *Buggy Breakout*

#26 *Camp Creepy*

#27 *Cat Burglar Caper*

#28 *Time Thief*

#29 *Designed for Disaster*

#30 *Dance off*

#31 *Make-a-Pet Mystery*

#32 *Cape Mermaid Mystery*

#33 *The Pumpkin Patch Puzzle*

#34 *Cupcake Chaos*

Nancy Drew and the Clue Crew®

#35

Cooking Camp Disaster

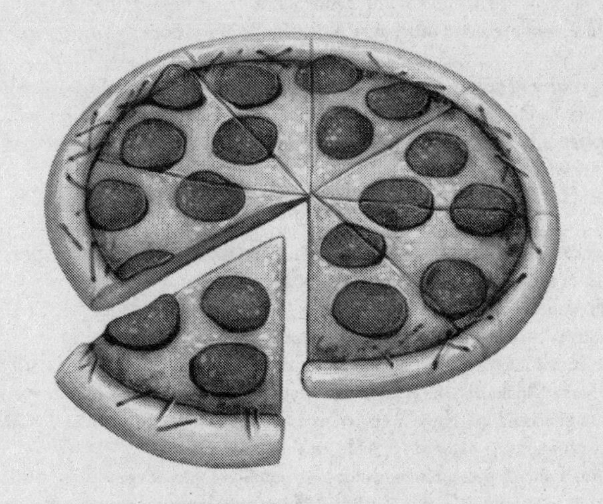

By Carolyn Keene

Illustrated by Macky Pamintuan

Aladdin
New York London Toronto Sydney New Delhi

ALADDIN
An imprint of Simon & Schuster Children's Publishing Division
1230 Avenue of the Americas, New York, NY 10020
First Aladdin paperback edition July 2013

Designed by Lisa Vega and Karina Granda
The text of this book was set in ITC Stone Informal.
Manufactured in the United States of America 0814 OFF
10 9 8 7 6 5 4 3
Library of Congress Catalog Card Number 2013938687
ISBN 978-1-4169-9466-4
ISBN 978-1-4424-8122-0 (eBook)

Contents

CHAPTER ONE

Off to Cooking Camp

"I've never been to a cooking camp before," said eight-year-old Nancy Drew. She peered out the car window eagerly.

"Me neither. I wonder what we'll learn to cook," her friend George Fayne added.

"I hope it's cupcakes. They're my favorite!" George's cousin Bess Marvin chimed in.

"Well, if it's cupcakes, make sure to save a couple for me," Hannah Gruen called out cheerfully from the driver's seat. The Drews' longtime housekeeper, Hannah had helped take care of Nancy from the time she was three. This morning she was driving the girls to camp. "Okay, here we are! As soon as I find a place to park, we can get you ladies settled in."

Nancy, George, and Bess were spending a week at Kid Kuisine, a summer day camp just outside their hometown of River Heights. As Hannah pulled into the driveway, Nancy craned her neck to see outside. The main building reminded her of a gingerbread house, with candy-colored shutters and flowering window boxes. The sprawling yard was filled with apple trees, gardens, and a pond.

A big sign near the front door read: WELCOME TO KID KUISINE! On it were hand-painted pictures of cookies, pizza, and fruits and vegetables.

This is going to be so cool! Nancy thought excitedly.

Hannah led Nancy, George, and Bess inside and handed their forms to an older girl sitting at the front desk. The girl had shoulder-length brown hair and chunky black glasses; her name tag said ROSEMARY.

Rosemary squinted at their forms. "Okay, so,

um, welcome, Nancy, Bess, and Georgia—"

"George," George corrected her.

"Sorry. George. Everyone's in the kitchen." Rosemary lifted her arm to direct them and accidentally knocked down a container full of pens and pencils. "Oops! Why am I *always* doing that?"

While Rosemary picked up the pens and pencils, Hannah gave Nancy a quick hug. "I'll see you girls later. Have fun!"

"Thanks, Hannah!" Nancy said, hugging her back.

Nancy and her friends headed through an arched doorway into the kitchen. It was a large, sunny room that was way bigger than Nancy's kitchen at home. Along the walls were several fancy-looking silver refrigerators as well as shelves filled with bottles, boxes, and jars of ingredients. In the middle of the room was an enormous island with sinks and counter space. Copper pots and pans hung from the ceilings, gleaming brightly.

There were six kids—three boys, three girls—sitting on stools around the island. A tall, bald man was showing one of the girls how to hold a wooden spoon properly.

The man beamed at Nancy, George, and Bess. "*Magnifico!* You must be our last three campers! I am Chef Giorgio, your instructor in the art of fine cooking!"

"Chef Giorgio? That sounds like my name, George," George said with a smile.

"I will have to call you Little Giorgio, then," Chef Giorgio said merrily. "Come in, please, and find some empty seats. Now that we're all here, we can go around and introduce ourselves."

Nancy and her friends sat down. The girl from the front desk, Rosemary, wandered into the kitchen just then and began rearranging a rack of spices. Her eyes flicked anxiously in Chef

Giorgio's direction. Nancy wondered why she seemed nervous.

"Okay, so why don't we all go around the room, say our names, and tell us a little something about yourselves?" Chef Giorgio suggested. "You can go first," he said to the girl with the wooden spoon.

"Me? Oh!" The girl sat up very straight. She had long, curly red hair and freckles. "I'm Chloe O'Malley! I'm eight years old! My favorite food is pizza! I have a dog named Lola, and she loves pizza too!"

"Lola is *not* your dog, she's *mine,*" the girl next to her said in a snotty voice. "I'm Cristin O'Malley," she said to everyone else. "I'm ten years old, and I can do a front *and* straddle split. Oh, and I have the biggest City Girls collection of anyone in my whole entire school."

"*Grazie,* Chloe and Cristin. That means 'thank you' in Italian. Okay, next? How about you?" Chef Giorgio gestured to a boy sitting across from the two sisters. He had scruffy blond hair and glasses and a T-shirt that said: GENIUS AT WORK.

"My name is Jeremy Kline. I'm ten, and I already know how to cook perfectly," he said matter-of-factly.

"*Magnifico!* You'll be a valuable addition to our little class, then," Chef Giorgio said. "How about you? Have you done any cooking before?" he asked the boy next to Jeremy.

"Uh, yeah. I like to mix ketchup and orange juice and feed it to my little sister. It gives her

a wicked stomachache," the boy said, grinning. "Oh, and I'm Dev Kapoor, by the way."

"Ketchup and orange juice? *Ew*," Bess whispered to Nancy.

The boy next to Dev gave him a high five. "Dude, I'm all over that recipe!"

"And what's your name?" Chef Giorgio asked him.

"Dylan. Dylan Wong. You can all call me Mr. Wong," he joked.

Nancy, George, and Bess introduced themselves next. When they were done, Chef Giorgio pointed to a girl sitting to the right of Nancy. She was wearing a pretty red dress with flowers. "And you? Tell us about yourself."

The girl squirmed in her seat. "Who, me? I'm Talisha. Talisha Nadine Eggers. I'm eight, and I . . . well . . . I don't know really know how to cook," she said quietly.

"Well, you will be an expert by the time this week is over!" Chef Giorgio said. "Okay, then. Let's get started with our class. We have some basics to go over first. Rosemary, will you please hand out some aprons to our students?"

While Rosemary did this, Chef Giorgio went over a bunch of safety rules, like how to handle the ovens, burners, and knives and other sharp utensils. He added that each camper would have his or her own workstation, with a sink, counter space, and so forth.

"Every day, you will learn to make a delicious new recipe," Chef Giorgio said. "And this Friday, which will be the last day of camp, there will be a very special event. We are going to—"

Chef Giorgio was interrupted by a very loud whirring noise. A moment later, someone screamed, *"Help!"*

CHAPTER TWO

The Brownie Fiasco

Nancy glanced quickly around the kitchen. Who was in trouble?

Across the island, Dev and Dylan were cracking up. They had turned on one of the blenders; it was causing the loud whirring noise. Dev was pushing buttons, making the blender go from low to medium to high. Dylan was dangling his hand over the top of the blender and pretend screaming, as though his fingers had gotten chopped off.

"Boys! Stop that right this instant!" Chef Giorgio rushed across the kitchen and shut off the blender. "I will not tolerate shenanigans. Please behave, or you will be asked to leave this camp!"

"We are super, super sorry," Dev said with a straight face.

"Yeah, we feel really, really bad about this," Dylan added. Nancy wondered if they were serious or just faking—again.

Bess turned to Nancy. "For a moment, I thought this was going to be a new case for the Clue Crew," she said in a low voice.

Talisha, who was sitting on the other side of Nancy, leaned over. "The Clue Crew? What's that?" she asked curiously.

"George, Bess, and I have a club called the

Clue Crew. We solve mysteries," Nancy explained to Talisha.

Talisha's eyes grew big. "Oh! That sounds cool!"

Chef Giorgio returned to his place in front of the group. "All right, let us move on. What was I saying? Oh, yes. We will have a special event on the last day of camp. First, you will all prepare a gourmet lunch and invite your parents and any other special guests you wish to include. And second, I will be awarding a prize for Best Chef!"

"You mean like a contest?" Cristin said.

"Yes, like a contest! I will decide who did the best job of making our recipes every day. And on Friday, I will announce the winner and give out a prize," Chef Giorgio explained.

"Maybe one of us will win," George whispered excitedly to Nancy and Bess.

"I wonder what the prize will be?" Bess whispered back.

Chef Giorgio went over a few more details about the week's activities. He added that there would be a second session of camp starting next Monday, for anyone who might want to come back for another week of cooking. "Now I will show you around the rest of our *magnifico* camp," he announced. "After that, we will return here to the kitchen to make our first recipe: peppermint brownies!"

Yum! Nancy thought. She and Hannah sometimes made brownies at home, but they'd never made peppermint brownies.

Chef Giorgio began his tour. First he showed everyone the big dining hall where they would be having their final-day banquet. Then he showed them the grounds. There were several gardens, including an herb garden and a vegetable garden. The vegetable garden had tomatoes, peppers, and sugar snap peas, among others. Nancy loved sugar snap peas, especially when Hannah cooked them with lots of butter!

After the tour, the group returned to the kitchen to make the peppermint brownies. Chef Giorgio listed the ingredients on a blackboard and demonstrated each step of the cooking process.

Rosemary went around helping everyone melt bittersweet chocolate pieces and margarine on the stove. While the mixture cooled, the students mixed sugar, eggs, vanilla, and cocoa powder in big mixing bowls.

"I'm definitely going to win Best Chef," Jeremy, the boy with the GENIUS AT WORK T-shirt, said to no one in particular. He poured two cups of sugar into his bowl. "I know pretty much everything there is to know about cooking. I do it all the time at home."

"Well, my mom's a caterer, so I know a lot about cooking too," George said as she poured sugar into her bowl.

"That's nice. You'll probably come in second place, then," Jeremy said.

"There *is* no second place," George pointed out.

Jeremy shrugged. "Too bad for you, then."

George turned and made a face at Nancy. She was obviously not happy about Mr. Show-Off.

Nancy smiled sympathetically at her friend. So far the boys at the camp were turning out to be not very nice.

After a picnic lunch outside, everyone returned to the kitchen to put the finishing touches on their peppermint brownies. Then Chef Giorgio walked around tasting samples.

"Mmm, *magnifico*!" he said to Chloe, who blushed and grinned with pleasure. "Yes, very good, but perhaps a touch less flour next time," he said to Cristin.

He reached George's workstation. "Little Giorgio! Let's see what you have created!" he said with a big smile.

George cut into her pan of brownies and handed the chef a big piece. He popped it into his mouth . . .

. . . and his smile instantly vanished. "*Yuck!* This is the worst peppermint brownie I have ever tasted!" he cried.

Chapter Three

Too Hot to Handle

George's face fell. "What do you mean, Chef Giorgio?" she said miserably.

"Here, taste!" Chef Giorgio broke off a piece of his peppermint brownie and thrust it at her.

George took a bite. "*Yuck!* You're right! It's supersalty!"

"Supersalty?" Nancy repeated. That didn't make sense. A teaspoon of salt was one of the ingredients in the recipe. But a teaspoon was hardly enough to make the brownies taste supersalty.

"*You* try it," George said, handing the brownie to Nancy.

Nancy bit into it cautiously. "Ew, definitely

salty," she said, scrunching up her face.

Puzzled, Nancy leaned over to George's work-station and peered at the salt jar. It was tall and clear, and it had a masking-tape label that said "Salt" on it. There was a tiny red smudge next to the word "Salt."

Beside it was an identical jar containing sugar. It had a masking-tape label that said "Sugar" on it. This label had a tiny red smudge too.

Then Nancy noticed something else. The labels were slightly crooked, as though they had been slapped on hastily. The labels on her own jars were *not* crooked. Neither were the labels on Bess's jars.

Acting on a hunch, Nancy opened George's salt jar and dipped her finger inside for a taste. When she licked her finger, she realized that the salt jar contained sugar. She did the same thing with the jar marked "Sugar." Likewise, the sugar jar contained salt.

"Your sugar jar has salt in it, and your salt jar has sugar in it," Nancy announced to

George. "You must have put two cups of salt into your peppermint brownie batter instead of sugar!"

"No way!" George exclaimed. "No wonder my brownies taste so gross."

Chef Giorgio pointed to Rosemary. "This is obviously your fault. You must have put the labels on wrong. You are always mixing things up!"

Rosemary gasped. "What? No way! I didn't do that, I swear!"

"We'll discuss this later. In the meantime,

I must finish tasting everyone's peppermint brownies," Chef Giorgio said testily.

Rosemary cheeks turned beet red. She looked nervous and embarrassed. Nancy wondered if Chef Giorgio was right. Did Rosemary simply make a mistake?

Just then, Nancy saw that Jeremy was staring at George over the top of his glasses and smiling smugly. Could *he* have switched the labels to mess up George's peppermint brownies? Or was he just gloating over her bad luck?

"Can I borrow some tomato sauce? I want to make my pizza extra tomato-y!" Bess called out to Nancy.

"Sure! I'm going to make *my* pizza extra cheesy," Nancy said, passing the tomato sauce to Bess.

It was Tuesday morning. Today's assignment was making pizzas to eat for lunch. It was great fun stretching the soft, pillowy pizza dough. Nancy also loved putting different ingredients on top. She even made a smiley-face design with a bunch of pepperoni pieces.

But not everyone seemed to be having a good time. Across the island, Cristin and her sister Chloe were arguing.

"Your pizza looks like Lola's throw-up!" Cristin was saying.

"My pizza does *not* look like Lola's throw-up! I'm telling Mom!" Chloe protested.

"Crybaby!"

"*You're* a crybaby!"

"Girls, girls, let's calm down," Chef Giorgio called out. "I think we could all use a little break. Why don't we go outside and pick some fresh herbs for our pizzas?"

Nancy, George, Bess, Chloe, Dev, and Dylan stopped what they were doing and followed Chef Giorgio out the door. Talisha, Cristin, Rosemary, and Jeremy stayed behind to go to the restroom first.

Outside in the herb garden, Nancy went up to Chloe. "Are you okay?" she asked her.

Chloe sniffed. "I'm okay. My sister can be supermean. But I guess sisters are like that. Do *you* have a sister?"

Nancy shook her head.

"Well, you can have mine if you want," Chloe said. "I'm just kidding! She can be nice sometimes. Like, she gave me a pink soccer ball for my birthday. Pink's my favorite color!"

"Did you say 'soccer'?"

Nancy turned around. Talisha was hovering

nearby. She, Cristin, Jeremy, and Rosemary had caught up to the rest of the group and were picking herbs.

"I love soccer," Talisha went on, smiling shyly. "When I grow up, I want to be a soccer player."

"That sounds cool," Chloe said. "I want to be a fashion designer. Or a veterinarian. Or maybe a chef."

"Why, so everyone can eat your dog-vomit food?" Cristin said as she passed by with a bunch of basil leaves.

Chloe gasped. "I am *so* telling Mom you said that! You're going to be grounded forever!"

"*You're* going to be grounded forever!"

"Girls!" Chef Giorgio rubbed his temples. "Am I going to have to separate you two again?"

Back in the kitchen, Chef Giorgio and Rosemary helped put everyone's pizzas in the very hot ovens to bake. Nancy loved the smell of the pizzas cooking. It was like being in an Italian restaurant!

Twenty minutes later, the pizzas were done, and the kids chopped fresh basil and oregano leaves from the herb garden to put on top. Then came the best part: lunchtime! Nancy couldn't wait to sit down and taste her pizza.

Rosemary passed out plates, napkins, forks, knives, and cups of water. Everyone sat down on their stools and prepared to chow down.

Nancy picked up a gooey slice and bit into it. *"Ow!"* she cried. Her mouth was on fire. Her pizza was the spiciest thing she'd ever eaten!

Chapter Four

A New Case

The other kids began crying out in pain too. Nancy grabbed her cup of water and downed it in one gulp.

"I don't understand. Is there something wrong with the pizzas?" Chef Giorgio said, sounding concerned.

"Yes! *Hot!*" Bess said with a gasp, pointing to her mouth.

"*Super*hot!" George agreed.

While the kids guzzled water, Chef Giorgio went around the kitchen inspecting and tasting everyone's pizzas. After a few minutes, he said, "There are red pepper flakes on all these pizzas. How could this be?"

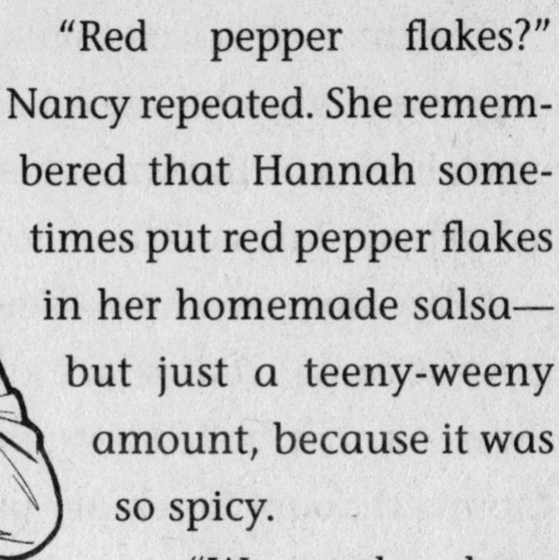

"Red pepper flakes?" Nancy repeated. She remembered that Hannah sometimes put red pepper flakes in her homemade salsa—but just a teeny-weeny amount, because it was so spicy.

"We only keep one bottle of red pepper flakes in our kitchen because we hardly ever use it," Chef Giorgio said. "Rosemary, please check the pantry to see if it's there. Go, hurry!"

"Yes, Chef," Rosemary said, scurrying away.

A moment later, she was back. "It's not there," she announced. "The bottle is missing!"

"This is two days in a row of weird stuff going on," Nancy said to George and Bess in a low voice. "Today it was the red pepper flakes. And yesterday, George, someone switched your salt and sugar jars."

The three girls were making a second batch of pizzas along with the other campers. The first batch had to be thrown out because they all had red pepper flakes on them.

"How do you know someone switched my jars?" George said as she arranged pineapple slices on her rolled-out pizza dough. "Chef Giorgio thought Rosemary probably just mixed up the labels by accident."

"Maybe. I noticed something funny, though," Nancy piped up. "The labels on your jars had these little red smudges on them."

"Really? What were they?" Bess said.

"I'm not sure. Mine didn't have them, and neither did yours, Bess." Nancy glanced around the kitchen. "We should look around and see if anyone else's labels have those smudges."

"Um, are you guys discussing your mystery?" Talisha said suddenly. She was shredding cheese at her workstation, to the right of Nancy's. She seemed to be having a hard time; the cheese was spilling everywhere. "Did you solve it yet?"

"Not exactly," Nancy said. "We're not sure if there *is* a mystery."

"I heard you talking about those red smudges. Maybe they're fingerprints?" Talisha suggested.

"Hmm, maybe," Nancy said.

"But why would they be red?" George pointed out.

"Because, um . . . hey, where did it go?" Talisha said, glancing around.

"Where did what go, Talisha?" Bess asked her.

"Chef Giorgio! Chef Giorgio!"

Nancy glanced up at the commotion. Cristin was waving her hand wildly and trying to get Chef Giorgio's attention.

Chef Giorgio was showing Dev how to chop mushrooms. "What is it, Cristin?" he called out.

"I know who put the red pepper flakes on our pizzas," Cristin announced. "It was my sister, Chloe!"

Chapter Five

The First Suspects

Chloe gasped. "Wh-what? I did not *put* red pepper flakes on everyone's pizzas!" she stammered.

"You did too! I have proof!" Cristin insisted.

"What proof?" Chef Giorgio demanded.

Cristin marched over to the row of backpacks hanging on the wall. Most of the backpacks had their owners' names or initials on them: DK, TNE, Dylan Wong, Jeremy, and so forth.

Cristin pointed to a pink backpack with Chloe's name on it. A small plastic bottle was sticking out of a side pocket. The bottle had a red cap.

Chef Giorgio walked over to the backpack and pulled out the bottle. "Red pepper flakes,"

he said gravely. "Chloe, what is the meaning of this?"

"But . . . but . . . I didn't put that there," Chloe blurted out. "I'm innocent!"

"Well, if you didn't put it there, then how did it get there?" Chef Giorgio pointed out. "It seems we have a mystery on our hands."

Dev whispered something in Dylan's ear,

and the two boys cracked up. Nancy frowned. Did *they* put the red pepper flakes in Chloe's backpack?

"Who needs a snack?" Hannah said merrily. She balanced a tray in her hands as she walked into Nancy's room.

"I'm superfull from camp!" Nancy said, patting her stomach.

"Me too," George added.

"Well . . . maybe just a tiny snack," Bess said with a grin.

Hannah set the tray down on the desk and left. It was late Tuesday afternoon, and the three girls were hanging out at Nancy's house. They had decided it would be a good idea to have an official Clue Crew meeting to discuss what was going on at camp. Nancy's puppy, Chocolate Chip, was curled up on the bed, taking a nap.

Nancy got her special detective notebook out of her desk drawer. George booted up Nancy's computer. Nancy liked to write down clues and suspects in the notebook while George typed up the information.

"Okay, let's start with suspects," Nancy said, uncapping her pen. "Who could have switched George's salt and sugar labels? And ruined everyone's pizzas?"

"Jeremy!" George said immediately. "J-E-R-E-M-Y," she spelled out loud as she typed. "He really wants to win Best Chef. Maybe he's worried I'll beat him, so he decided to destroy my peppermint brownies."

"What about Dev and Dylan?" Bess said, grabbing a fistful of popcorn from the tray. "They did that dumb thing with the blender yesterday. They're really into pranks!"

Nancy wrote down the three boys' names. "I guess we should add Chloe, too, because of the red pepper flakes," she mused. "The thing is . . . whoever put the red pepper flakes on the pizzas probably did it while we were outside picking basil and stuff, right?"

"Right," George agreed.

"That's the problem. Chloe was with us that whole time. I know, because she and I were talking," Nancy said.

"Oh! That *is* a problem." George looked thoughtful. "I remember that a few kids stayed inside to go to the bathroom. They came outside a few minutes after everyone else."

"Enough time to sprinkle red pepper flakes on everyone's pizzas?" Bess said.

"Maybe. So who went to the bathroom?" Nancy scrunched up her face, trying to remember. "Jeremy . . . and Talisha . . ."

"And Cristin. Oh, and Rosemary, too," George said, typing.

"But the red pepper flakes bottle was in Chloe's backpack," Nancy said. "Unless someone put it in there to make Chloe look guilty?"

While George entered everything on the computer, Nancy read over what she'd written in her notebook so far:

SUSPECTS

Jeremy: He wants to win the Best Chef prize. He went to the bathroom for a few minutes while everyone was outside picking herbs. So he had time to put red pepper flakes on the pizzas.

Dev and Dylan: They like to pull pranks and break rules. BUT they were outside picking herbs. So they didn't have time to put red pepper flakes on the pizzas.

Chloe: The bottle of red pepper flakes was in her backpack. BUT she was outside picking herbs the whole time too.

Nancy glanced up from the notebook. "What about clues?" she said. "There's the bottle of red pepper flakes in Chloe's backpack. Plus, there's the weird red smudges on your salt and sugar jars, George."

"They weren't on anyone else's jars," George said. "I went around and checked this morning."

"Hmm. That's good to know!" Nancy picked up her pen again and wrote:

CLUES

> The bottle of red pepper flakes was in Chloe's backpack.
>
> The "Salt" and "Sugar" labels on George's jars were switched. They were kind of crooked. And they had little red smudge marks on them.

Nancy nibbled on her pen. What if the two incidents weren't even related? What if one person messed up George's peppermint brownies and another person messed up all the pizzas?

Maybe the Clue Crew had *two* culprits to catch.

Chapter Six

The Clueless Crew?

"The trick to decorating a cake is planning in advance," Chef Giorgio said. "Decide what you're going to put on your cake first. Make a little drawing, even. Arrange all your ingredients: icing, powdered sugar, little candies, cut-up fruit, edible flowers, and so forth. Then . . . decorate!"

It was Wednesday morning, and Chef Giorgio was teaching the campers how to decorate a cake. He and Rosemary had baked a bunch of round yellow cakes the night before. Now it was up to the kids to add the finishing touches.

Nancy had decided to decorate her cake with an ocean theme. Following Chef Giorgio's advice, she first drew a picture of sea creatures such as dolphins, jellyfish, sharks, and whales. She added a background of blue water as well as coral, seashells, and seaweed.

George was going to decorate her cake with a soccer theme. Bess's theme was ballet.

"Ugh! This is *hard*!"

Nancy glanced to her right. Talisha seemed to be having a tough time with her cake. She was trying to make a swirly design with a tube of red icing. But the icing was splattering this way and that. Her workstation was a big red mess!

"Maybe you're squeezing the tube too hard?" Nancy said gently.

"This is so not fun," Talisha moaned.

Rosemary came up to Talisha, wiping her hands on her apron. "I can help you with that! Don't worry about making it perfect. I used to be superawkward with cake decorating too. It just takes a little practice."

"No, Rosemary, you *still* don't know how to do it properly. *I* will help Talisha. You can go wash up those dishes in the sink," Chef Giorgio interrupted.

Rosemary hung her head. "Yes, Chef," she mumbled.

Nancy wondered why Chef Giorgio was always mean to Rosemary. He was so nice to everyone else.

Nancy turned her attention back to her cake. It was almost done; she just had a couple of fish to "draw" with icing.

As she worked, she glanced around the kitchen. She wished she could figure out who was responsible for George's salty peppermint brownies as well as the superspicy pizzas. So far, the Clue Crew had four suspects on their list: Jeremy, Dev, Dylan, and Chloe. Nancy really wanted to talk to all of them as soon as possible and try to get more information from them.

She noticed that Jeremy was checking out her cake from across the island.

"Hmm, not bad," he called out. "It's better

than George's or Bess's. It's still not as good as mine, though. I'm definitely going to win Best Chef on Friday!"

Jeremy's cake had a space theme. It had stars, moons, planets, and rockets on it, and a scary-looking alien, too.

"Well, at least I don't have to cheat to win," George snapped at Jeremy.

"Cheat? What are you talking about?" Jeremy asked her.

"You switched my salt and sugar jars so my peppermint brownies would be supersalty. And I bet you put red pepper flakes on everyone's pizzas, too!" George blurted out.

"The Clue Crew is on the case. If you're guilty, we'll catch you!" Bess added.

"The Clue *what*?" Jeremy said.

"The Clue Crew. Nancy and George and I solve mysteries," Bess explained huffily.

Jeremy pushed his glasses up his nose. "I don't need to cheat to win Best Chef," he said with a mean smile. "Besides, even if I *did* cheat, I'm too smart to be caught by you, Clueless Crew!"

After a picnic lunch outside in the warm summer sun, everyone met back in the kitchen to finish decorating their cakes. Nancy and Bess were done before everyone else. They began putting their unused ingredients back in the big refrigerator in the corner of the room.

They passed Cristin's and Chloe's workstations. As usual, the two sisters were arguing.

"Your cake looks like messed-up spaghetti!" Cristin said to Chloe.

"Well, *your* cake looks like yucky garbage!" Chloe shot back.

Nancy and Bess exchanged a glance. Nancy was about to say something when she heard a voice calling out to them. "Hey, you! Uh, Crew Cuts! Over here!"

Dev was waving to them. He and Dylan were decorating a cake together.

Nancy and Bess walked over to their workstation. "We're not the *Crew Cuts*. We're the *Clue Crew*. What do you want?" Bess asked them, sounding annoyed.

"We need your help," Dylan said, handing Bess a measuring cup. "Could you pour this into the middle of our cake? Dev and I have to pour powdered sugar and chocolate chips on the cake at the exact same time. So, uh, we need a third person."

Nancy peered curiously at the measuring

cup. It had some sort of clear liquid in it. It had a strong, strange smell. But she couldn't figure out what it was. Chef Giorgio paused at the workstation, then moved on to Talisha's.

Nancy's gaze fell on the cake. It was different from the cakes all the other campers were working on. For one thing, it wasn't small and round. It was tall and kind of cone-shaped, with a hole on top.

Bess took the measuring cup from Dylan and started to tip it over the cake.

"No, Bess! *Stop!*" Nancy cried out suddenly.

Chapter Seven

The Almost-Exploding Volcano Cake

Bess jerked back, nearly dropping the measuring cup. But fortunately the liquid didn't spill onto the cake.

"Wh-why did you tell me to stop, Nancy?" Bess stammered.

"That's not a cake. It's a baking-soda volcano!" Nancy explained. "Remember? Someone made one of those for the school science fair last year. The measuring cup has vinegar in it. If you pour it into the volcano, it mixes with the baking soda inside and start bubbling and erupting like crazy!"

Bess's eyes grew enormous. "Oh my gosh! You're right!"

Dev and Dylan cracked up.

Bess glared at the two boys. "Yeah, very funny! It's almost as funny as the other dumb stuff you did. Like destroying George's peppermint brownies and everyone's pizzas!"

"Huh? We totally didn't do that stuff," Dev said.

"Yeah, but I wish we did!" Dylan added.

Nancy regarded them suspiciously. "Where did this volcano come from?" she asked them.

"We made it at Dylan's house last night and brought it in this morning," Dev said. "We thought it would be a superfunny prank!"

Nancy glanced across the kitchen. Chef Giorgio was busy helping Talisha with her cake. He didn't seem to notice what was going on at Dev and Dylan's workstation.

Chef Giorgio had told Dev and Dylan on Monday that if they continued with their bad behavior, they would have to leave the camp. She wondered if she and Bess should tell Chef Giorgio about the volcano, or if they should give the boys another chance.

Because if Dev and Dylan left the camp, and if it turned out they *were* responsible for messing up the brownies and pizzas, the Clue Crew would never know!

"Are you girls ready to go?" Hannah said.

Camp was over for the day, and Hannah was waiting outside the front door. She had promised to take Nancy, George, and Bess to the mall and then home to the Drews' house for make-your-own-taco night.

"Hi, Hannah! We're ready!" Nancy adjusted her backpack on her shoulder and rushed up to Hannah, hugging her. She wiped a bead of sweat from her brow. Although it was late in the day, it was blazing hot outside. Even the herbs in the herb garden looked a little wilted from the heat.

"That Jeremy is *so* guilty. We're *this* close to catching him!" George grumbled to Bess as they caught up to Nancy and Hannah.

"Yeah, but what about Dev and Dylan?

That volcano trick was definitely not cool," Bess complained.

"Yeah, but I think Jeremy is the one who—wait, where's my backpack?" George stopped in her tracks and glanced around, frowning. "Sorry, guys. I think I forgot it inside."

"Let's all go in. I could use a drink of water, anyway," Hannah said.

The four of them headed back into the building. The other campers had already left with their parents and babysitters. Nancy knew that Rosemary was still around, though; she'd seen her just a few minutes ago. She wasn't sure about Chef Giorgio.

Nancy led the way to the kitchen. She paused at the doorway; she could see George's backpack across the room, hanging on its usual hook.

Then she saw something else—something odd. She put her finger to her lips, indicating to George, Bess, and Hannah that they should be quiet.

Rosemary was standing at the island, her

back to the door. On the counter in front of her were the campers' decorated cakes: nine in all.

Rosemary was holding a tube of icing over one of the cakes. Nancy leaned forward to get a better look. Was Rosemary about to mess up that cake?

Could *she* be the culprit?

Chapter Eight

Too Many Suspects

"What's going on?" George whispered to Nancy.

Nancy pointed to Rosemary, who was still holding the icing tube over the cake. She was muttering softly to herself and making swirly patterns in the air, above the cake.

"Maybe *she's* the one who's been messing everything up," Nancy whispered back. "It kind of makes sense. Chef Giorgio's pretty mean to her. What if she's trying to get back at him?"

"Yes! And we can prove it!" Bess pointed out.

"How?" Hannah piped up. "My goodness, this is very exciting! I'm at the crime scene! That's what you detectives call it, right? Or is it 'the scene of the crime'?"

Bess didn't answer Hannah, but instead marched boldly into the kitchen. "Aha!" she announced to Rosemary. "We caught you red-handed! You're our criminal!"

Rosemary whirled around. She dropped the icing tube on the floor. "Wh-what? What are you talking about?" she stammered.

"You were just about to destroy somebody's cake!" Bess went on. "What's in that tube? Red pepper flakes? You're the one who ruined George's

peppermint brownies Monday, aren't you? And all our pizzas yesterday?"

"What? No!" Rosemary bent down and picked up the icing tube from the floor. "This is Talisha's cake. I wasn't about to destroy it! I wasn't even decorating it; I was just pretending to."

"Why would you do that?" Nancy asked her.

"Because Chef Giorgio never lets me cook!" Rosemary said, pouting. "I took this job so I could become a celebrity chef someday. I thought this

would be a good place for me to learn how to cook. But Chef Giorgio makes me wash dishes and mop floors and stuff all the time. He only hired me because my aunt Petunia is BFFs with his mom, and his mom convinced him to give me a job. He doesn't like me!"

"Why not?" George said.

Rosemary shrugged. "I don't know! He says I'm incompetent. Like, I don't know what I'm doing. But I *do* know what I'm doing. It's just that he makes me so nervous that I'm always dropping stuff and mixing stuff up!"

Nancy thought for a moment. "So . . . did you maybe mix up the salt and sugar labels on George's jars? By accident?"

Rosemary shook her head. "Definitely not! I double-checked those labels right after I put them on." She added, "Chef Giorgio had to leave early today to run errands. He asked me to close up. Please, please don't tell him I was in here pretending to decorate cakes! He'd be so mad at me, even though I didn't do anything wrong. He's the meanest boss ever!"

Nancy, George, and Bess exchanged a glance. Nancy wondered: Was Rosemary telling the truth? Or was her story a fancy, complicated cover-up?

"Yum! Pass the guacamole, please!" Bess said.

"I love make-your-own-taco night!" George chimed in.

"Me too!" Nancy agreed.

It was Wednesday night. The girls had spent an hour at the mall with Hannah, shopping. Now they were at the Drews' house having tacos with Hannah and Nancy's father, Carson Drew.

"So Hannah tells me the Clue Crew is working on a new mystery," Carson said to Nancy and her friends. "Can you talk about it? Or is it top secret?"

"We can tell *you* about it, Daddy," Nancy said with a smile.

"As long as you promise you won't tell anyone else," Bess added.

Carson crossed his heart. "I promise!"

Nancy proceeded to fill her father in on the details of the case. Carson was a lawyer, and he sometimes gave the Clue Crew advice on their detective work.

When Nancy was finished, Carson looked thoughtful. "Hmm. Sounds like you girls have a real puzzle on your hands," he mused.

"We do!" Bess said. She bit into her taco.

"So do you believe Chef Giorgio's assistant,

Rosemary?" Carson asked. "Was she just pretending to decorate the cake? Or was she actually about to sabotage it?" He added, "'Sabotage' is another word for 'mess up.'"

"We're not sure yet," Nancy replied, scooping some salsa onto her plate. "We only have two more days to solve the mystery. Friday is the last day of camp—and it's the big banquet, too! You're coming to that, right, Daddy? And Hannah?"

"I wouldn't miss it for the world, Pumpkin Pie," Carson said.

"Neither would I. And I know you girls will crack this case. You always do," Hannah told them.

After dinner Nancy, George, and Bess went up to Nancy's room. Nancy wanted to update their lists of suspects and clues.

George turned on Nancy's computer. Nancy got her detective notebook out of her desk drawer. Bess plopped down on Nancy's bed to pet Chocolate Chip, who was busily chewing one of Nancy's slippers.

"So I think we should add Rosemary to our suspect list," Nancy began.

"Definitely! I mean, she might have been telling the truth. But she might have been lying, too," George said.

George leaned over the keyboard and began typing. Nancy opened her notebook to the "suspects" page and added Rosemary to the list. She also updated a few other things:

SUSPECTS

Jeremy: He wants to win the Best Chef prize. He went to the bathroom for a few minutes while everyone was outside picking herbs. So he had time to put red pepper flakes on the pizzas. He bragged and said he was definitely going to win Best Chef. Plus, he bragged that if he cheated, the Clue Crew would never find out.

Dev and Dylan: They like to pull pranks and break rules. BUT they were outside picking herbs. So they didn't have time to put red pepper flakes on the pizzas. They almost pulled another prank, though—the volcano cake!

Chloe: The bottle of red pepper flakes was in her backpack. BUT she was outside picking herbs the whole time too.

Rosemary: We caught her maybe messing up Talisha's cake. She said she was just pretending to decorate it, though. Chef Giorgio is kind of mean to her. Maybe she wants to get revenge and cause trouble for his camp?

Nancy read over what she'd written. And read it a second time. And a third time. Their suspect list was getting very long.

She felt like she was overlooking something—something obvious. What could it be?

"Chloe!" Nancy said suddenly. "Bess, remember what you said yesterday? About how someone might have put the red pepper flakes bottle in her backpack?"

Bess nodded. "Uh-huh."

"What if it was Cristin?" Nancy said excitedly. "Maybe *she's* the culprit. And she was just trying to make Chloe look guilty!"

Chapter Nine

The Mysterious Fortune Cookie

"That makes sense," George said. "The two of them are *always* fighting."

"Like all the time!" Bess agreed.

"I think we should add Cristin to the suspect list, and take Chloe off," Nancy suggested.

"Good idea. And tomorrow, let's ask Cristin some questions. Maybe we can get her to crack," Bess said.

"Crack?" Nancy repeated, confused.

"That's detective talk for 'make her confess,'" Bess said, giggling.

But on Thursday, Cristin wasn't at camp. Chloe told everyone that she was staying home for the day because she had a doctor's appointment.

"So now we can't make Cristin crack," Bess complained in a low voice to Nancy and George.

Nancy, George, Bess, and the rest of the campers were preparing their workstations for the day's project: fortune cookies. Nancy was really psyched about this assignment. She and the others were going to write their own fortunes to put inside the cookies!

"Maybe she'll be here tomorrow. And we can still try to make our other suspects, um, crack today," Nancy said to Bess.

"Yeah. We still have Evil Jeremy, Dev and Dylan, and Rosemary," George pointed out.

"We're running out of time, though. Tomorrow's the last day of camp," Bess said worriedly.

Talisha leaned over to Nancy and the girls. "Are you guys talking about your mystery? Have you solved it yet?"

"Um, not yet," Nancy replied. She wondered why Talisha seemed so interested in their case.

"Have you thought about doing fingerprint

analy . . . analysis? Did I say that right? You could make everyone press their fingertips on an inkpad and then on a piece of paper!" Talisha suggested. "And what about witnesses? Maybe someone here saw or heard something suspipicious . . . I mean, suspicious!"

"Wow, are you a big mystery fan or what?" Bess asked her curiously.

Talisha blushed. "Yeah, kind of. I read a lot of mystery books. And I like mystery movies, too." She added, "I like mysteries almost as much as I like soccer!"

"Soccer's awesome," George agreed.

"It's the awesomest! I was supposed to go to soccer camp this summer. But my mom and dad made me do cooking camp instead. They said I needed to try something new." Talisha made a face.

"Cooking's fun too, right?" Bess said.

Talisha shrugged. "I guess. I don't know. I'd rather be playing soccer."

After lunch the campers met back inside the kitchen to snack on their fortune cookies. Before lunch they had all written their own messages on thin slivers of paper and put them into the folded, still-warm cookies. Now they were cool enough to eat.

Some of the kids traded cookies with each other, including Bess and George. When Bess opened hers, she started laughing. "Ha-ha! 'You will be a millionaire someday,'" she read out loud. "Yay!"

George opened hers. "'You will rule the universe!'" she read, grinning. "Yes!"

Nancy's fortune cookie was cooling on a small blue plate. But there was another fortune cookie sitting on her cutting board. It was bigger than hers and kind of lumpy-looking. She wasn't sure who had given it to her.

Nancy cracked it open. She gasped when she saw the bizarre message inside:

CHAPTER TEN

Buon Appetito!

Nancy stared at the strange message. She noticed that it was written in red ink. And there was a weird red smudge at the edge of the paper—a different, slightly lighter shade of red. It looked similar to the smudges that she'd seen on George's salt and sugar labels.

Nancy leaned over and showed the message to George and Bess. "What do you think it means?" she whispered.

"I guess someone really, really wants you—or us—to stop snooping." George squinted at the red smudge. "It's kind of shaped like a fingerprint. But it's kind of blurry, too."

Bess pointed to the words. "Why are some of the letters in the message capital letters?"

Nancy nodded slowly. The letters *T*, *N*, and *E* were capitalized. The rest of the letters were not. "Do you think it's some sort of code?" she said out loud.

"Or maybe it's the word 'ten,' mixed up," George suggested.

Nancy thought hard. *T, N, E.* What could those letters stand for? Was it the word "ten" scrambled around, like George said? Or was it something else?

The letters actually seemed familiar to her. She wasn't sure why. She had seen them before, in exactly that order . . .

Her gaze fell on the backpacks hanging up across the room. They were labeled with the campers' names and initials: DK, Dylan Wong, Jeremy, Chloe O., TNE . . .

TNE!

Nancy whirled around to face the workstation on her right. Talisha Nadine Eggers. TNE.

"Talisha! You left me this fortune cookie, didn't you? And you're the one the Clue Crew has been looking for!" Nancy said, surprised.

Talisha glanced up from washing out a bowl she had used to make the fortune-cookie batter. She had a big, happy smile on her face. "Uh-huh. Yay, you finally caught me! And now you can turn me in to Chef Giorgio!" she said eagerly.

"*You're* the one who messed up my peppermint brownies?" George cried out.

Talisha nodded. "Uh-huh. I'm really, really sorry! The three of you walked away for a minute to get something in the refrigerator. So I switched the salt and sugar labels really superfast, when no one was looking. Then I put strawberry jam on my fingers and left my fingerprints on the labels, so the Clue Crew would catch me right away!" She frowned. "Except, uh, you didn't."

"Wow. And did you mess up everyone's pizzas too?" Bess asked her.

"Yup! I even put the bottle of red pepper flakes *right here* in the middle of my cutting board! That way, I figured you would *definitely* catch me. But then it disappeared!" Talisha pointed to Chloe, who was on the other side of the kitchen munching on a fortune cookie. "I think that maybe her sister Cristin took it and put it into her backpack. To get her into trouble or whatever."

Nancy gazed at Chloe. That made sense, and

was pretty much what Nancy, George, and Bess had guessed, anyway.

But the rest of Talisha's confession made *zero* sense.

"I don't get it," Nancy said to Talisha. "Why did you try so hard to get caught? I mean, Chef Giorgio would have made you leave the camp!"

"But that's what I *wanted*!" Talisha insisted. "I never wanted to go to cooking camp. I wanted to go to soccer camp! I came up with my plan on Monday. Remember? When those boys Dev and Dylan did that blender thing? And Chef Giorgio told them they would get kicked out if they kept breaking the rules? Plus, you guys told me about your Clue Crew club? I figured I could break the rules too, and you'd catch me and turn me in to Chef Giorgio!"

"That's a crazy plan!" George said.

"Yeah, but it almost worked," Bess pointed out.

"Why did you give me this fortune-cookie message and tell me to stop snooping?" Nancy asked Talisha. "Tomorrow's the last day of camp.

It's too late to switch camps now, isn't it?"

"I *thought* it was. I was going to give up on my plan after the peppermint brownies and the pizza. But then last night Mom and Dad told me they were going to sign me up for another week of cooking camp, next week. I *had* to do something!" Talisha said.

"I understand why you wanted to go to soccer camp so badly, but you almost ruined cooking camp for everyone else this week," George pointed out.

Talisha hung her head. "Yeah. I know. I feel really badly about that. Maybe there's something I can do to make it up to all of you guys?"

"Mmm, this is delicious. What do you call it?" Carson asked Nancy.

"I call it the Clue Crew Calzone. It has cheese and sausage in it, plus a mystery ingredient!" Nancy said with a grin.

Hannah chuckled. "I guess you can't give me the recipe, then. It's top secret!"

It was Friday at lunchtime. The Kid Kuisine dining hall was filled with dozens of people: the nine campers, their parents, and other guests. The kids were serving everyone lunch with Rosemary's help. Chef Giorgio was at the door, greeting people as they came in.

Nancy, George, Bess, and the other campers had spent the morning cooking a gourmet feast. The menu included not-spicy pizza and also calzone, which was kind of like a folded-over pizza. For dessert, there were peppermint brownies—with no extra salt.

Talisha was serving pizza and calzone to her mom and dad, Mr. and Mrs. Eggers. Nancy was glad the mystery was finally solved. Talisha had told Chef Giorgio everything, and her parents, too. This morning Talisha had updated Nancy, George, and Bess, saying that her parents weren't going to make her come back to the second session of cooking camp, but that she wouldn't be able to go to soccer camp, either. Maybe later in the summer, after she'd spent a few weeks helping out at home and making up for what she'd done. In the meantime Talisha had baked cupcakes at home and brought them in for everyone, to say "I'm sorry" for what she'd done.

The event seemed to be a big success. The food was yummy. Dev and Dylan were behaving and not pulling any pranks. Chloe and Cristin weren't arguing, even though Nancy had confronted Cristin earlier about the bottle of red pepper flakes. Cristin had admitted to her and Chloe that she'd planted it in Chloe's backpack. Chloe had forgiven Cristin only after Cristin promised to give Chloe one of her City Girls dolls.

Even Rosemary seemed to be happier. That morning she had told Nancy, George, and Bess that Chef Giorgio had apologized to her last night for being so mean to her all the time. He had explained to her that the chef business was very tough and he was just trying to prepare her for what lay ahead.

"Excuse me! May I have your attention?"

Chef Giorgio was standing at a microphone near the doorway. "First of all, I want to thank all of you for being here today. I hope you're enjoying the children's *magnifico* food! *Buon appetito!*" he said loudly.

Everyone cheered.

"Second of all, I want to announce the winner of our Best Chef contest. This award goes to the camper who made the most successful recipes this week. The prize is a gift certificate for two at the Double Dip ice cream shop. And the prize goes to . . ." Chef Giorgio paused dramatically.

Nancy glanced around the room. Jeremy was smiling confidently at George and pointing to himself, like he was going to win. George was smiling confidently back at him and pointing to herself, like *she* was going to win.

"It's a tie! Our winners are Jeremy Kline and Little Giorgio!" said Chef Giorgio. "That's my nickname for George Fayne," he added.

Everyone clapped. George looked shocked. So did Jeremy.

"Wow, lucky you! You get to go to the Double Dip with Jeremy!" Nancy teased George.

"Yeah, you're going to be best friends now," Bess joked.

"Um . . . uh . . ." George shrugged and laughed.

Nancy and Bess laughed too. Then the three friends sat down with their parents and Hannah and dug into some Clue Crew Calzones.

Mystery solved!

LET'S MAKE SOME BARK!

No, not the kind of bark that comes from trees! LOL! Nancy, George, and Bess love to make peppermint bark for dessert or a yummy afternoon snack. You can make peppermint bark at home too, with the help of a parent or other grown-up.

Here are the ingredients you will need:

1 pound milk chocolate (either bars or chips)
24 hard peppermint candies or mini candy canes
Cooking spray

You will also need the following equipment and supplies:

A 9x12-inch cookie sheet

Wax paper or parchment paper

A large microwavable bowl (for the chocolate)

A large Ziploc bag

A hammer or rolling pin

Now just follow these simple steps:

Spray cooking spray onto the cookie sheet. Then line the cookie sheet with a piece of wax paper or parchment paper. Make sure the paper hangs slightly over the long sides of the cookie sheet.

Ask a grown-up to help you melt the chocolate. Put the chocolate in a large microwavable bowl and microwave on medium for thirty seconds. Stir and check to see if it's melted; if not, repeat for another thirty seconds. Keep repeating this step until the chocolate is melted. Take the bowl out of the microwave and allow the chocolate to cool slightly. (OPTION: You can also melt the chocolate in a double boiler on the stove. Ask a grown-up to help you do this.)

Pour the melted chocolate onto the cookie sheet. Spread evenly with a spatula or wooden spoon.

Put the peppermint candies or mini candy canes in the Ziploc bag and seal. Ask a grown-up to help you smash the candies into little pieces with a hammer or rolling pin.

Spread the smashed-up candies on top of the melted chocolate.

Refrigerate for an hour or until the chocolate is hard.

Once the peppermint bark is hard, you can peel off the paper and break the bark up into uneven pieces.

VARIATIONS: You can experiment with different toppings for your bark. Try s'mores bark (put mini marshmallows and broken-up graham cracker pieces on top instead of peppermint candies or candy canes). Or try nuts 'n' berries bark (put different kinds of nuts and dried cranberries or raisins on top). Or any other kind of bark you can think of!

Buon appetito!

Nancy Drew and The Clue Crew

Test your detective skills with more Clue Crew cases!

#1 *Sleepover Sleuths*
#2 *Scream for Ice Cream*
#3 *Pony Problems*
#4 *The Cinderella Ballet Mystery*
#5 *Case of the Sneaky Snowman*
#6 *The Fashion Disaster*
#7 *The Circus Scare*
#8 *Lights, Camera . . . Cats!*
#9 *The Halloween Hoax*
#10 *Ticket Trouble*
#11 *Ski School Sneak*
#12 *Valentine's Day Secret*
#13 *Chick-napped!*
#14 *The Zoo Crew*
#15 *Mall Madness*
#16 *Thanksgiving Thief*
#17 *Wedding Day Disaster*
#18 *Earth Day Escapade*
#19 *April Fool's Day*
#20 *Treasure Trouble*
#21 *Double Take*
#22 *Unicorn Uproar*
#23 *Babysitting Bandit*
#24 *Princess Mix-up Mystery*
#25 *Buggy Breakout*
#26 *Camp Creepy*
#27 *Cat Burglar Caper*
#28 *Time Thief*
#29 *Designed for Disaster*
#30 *Dance Off*
#31 *The Make-a-Pet Mystery*
#32 *Cape Mermaid Mystery*
#33 *The Pumpkin Patch Puzzle*

FROM ALADDIN • PUBLISHED BY SIMON & SCHUSTER

Candy Fairies

Visit candyfairies.com for more delicious fun with your favorite fairies.

Play games, download activities, and so much more!

EBOOK EDITIONS ALSO AVAILABLE

FROM ALADDIN • KIDS.SIMONANDSCHUSTER.COM